WRITTEN AND ILLUSTRATED BY

## Cynthia Rylant

THE BLUE SKY PRESS

An Imprint of Scholastic Inc. • New York

# DOG

# HEAVEN

THE BLUE SKY PRESS

Copyright © 1995 by Cynthia Rylant
All rights reserved.
No part of this publication may be reproduced,
stored in a retrieval system, or transmitted in
any form or by any means, electronic, mechanical,
photocopying, recording, or otherwise, without
written permission of the publisher.
For information regarding permission,
please write to: Permissions Department,
Scholastic Inc., 557 Broadway, New York, New York 10012.
SCHOLASTIC, THE BLUE SKY PRESS, and associated logos
are trademarks and/or registered trademarks of Scholastic Inc.
Library of Congress Cataloging-in-Publication Data
Rylant, Cynthia. Dog heaven /
written and illustrated by Cynthia Rylant.
p.      cm.
Summary: God created Dog Heaven, a place
where dogs can eat ice-cream biscuits, sleep on
fluffy clouds, and run through unending fields.
ISBN-13: 978-0-590-41701-3 / ISBN-10: 0-590-41701-0
[1. Dogs — Fiction.    2. Heaven — Fiction.]    I. Title.
PZ7.R982Do    1995    [E] — dc20
94-40950    CIP    AC
50 49 48 47 46                              15 16 17/0
Printed in Malaysia 108
First printing, September 1995

FOR DIANE

**W**hen dogs go to Heaven,
they don't need wings
because God knows that
dogs love running best.

He gives them fields. Fields and fields and fields.

When a dog first arrives in Heaven,

he just runs.

Dog Heaven has clear, wide lakes
filled with geese who honk and flap
and tease. The dogs love this.

They run beside the water and bark
and bark and God watches them
from behind a tree and smiles.

There are children,
of course.
Angel children.

God knows that dogs love children more than anything else in the world, so He fills Dog Heaven with plenty of them. There are children on bikes and children on sleds. There are children throwing red rubber balls and children pulling kites through the clouds. The dogs are there, and the children love them dearly.

And, oh,
the dog biscuits.
Biscuits and biscuits
as far as the eye can see.

God has a sense of humor, so He makes His
biscuits in funny shapes for His dogs. There
are kitty-cat biscuits and squirrel biscuits.
Ice-cream biscuits and ham-sandwich biscuits.

Every angel who passes by
has a biscuit for a dog.

And, of course, all God's dogs
sit when the angels say "sit."

Every dog becomes a good
dog in Dog Heaven.

God turns
clouds inside out to
make fluffy beds for the dogs
in Dog Heaven, and when they
are tired from running and
barking and eating ham-
sandwich biscuits,

the dogs each find a cloud
bed for sleeping.

They turn around and
around in the cloud...

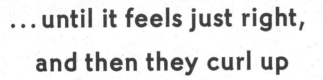

...until it feels just right,
and then they curl up

and they sleep.

God watches over each one of them and there are no bad dreams.

Dogs in Dog Heaven
have almost always
belonged to somebody
on Earth and, of course,
the dogs remember this.
Heaven is full of memories.

So sometimes an angel will walk a dog
back to Earth for a little visit and quietly,
invisibly, the dog will sniff about his old
backyard, will investigate the cat next
door, will follow the child to school, will
sit on the front porch and wait for the mail.

When he is satisfied

that all is well, the dog

will return to Heaven with the angel.

It is where dogs belong,

near God who made them.

The dogs in Dog Heaven who
had no real homes on Earth
are given one in Heaven.

The homes have yards and porches and there are couches to lie on and tables to sit under while angels eat their dinners.

There are special bowls with the dogs' names on them.

Abbey

And each dog is petted and reminded
how good he is, all day long.

Dogs in Dog Heaven may stay as long as
they like and this can mean forever.

They will be there when old friends show up. They will be there at the door.

Angel dogs.

The paintings in this book

were done with acrylics.

The text type was set in Martin Gothic Bold

and the display type in LoType Medium

by WLCR New York, Inc.

Color separations were made by

Bright Arts, Ltd., Singapore. Printed and

bound by Tien Wah Press, Singapore.

Production supervision by Angela Biola

Designed by Kathleen Westray